Chapter One

The ravens were swooping down from the skies as Andy ran by the river. He was sure they were going to attack him.

Suddenly one of the beaks stabbed his forehead. Another ripped at his hair. Yet another grazed his cheek and he was soon smarting with pain, the blood running into his eyes.

Andy fell, knuckles bleeding, curling up into a ball against the vicious attack.

Andy!

For a few minutes there was silence. The sky was black with circling ravens. Then they swooped again, beaks slashing.

Ravens' Revenge

Anthony Masters
Illustrated by Peter Dennis

A & C Black · London

Andy's mother looked down at her son in concern.

Greystone Grange was a ruined Victorian mansion with the canoe centre in the outbuildings.

When Andy arrived by taxi from the station he saw something in the clear blue July sky that gave him a nasty shock.

A raven was wheeling overhead in slow, graceful arcs. Then it was joined by another.

Andy shivered, remembering his nightmare.

That night, lying in his bunk bed, Andy dreamt of ravens yet again. They were flying over his head, making their mournful cawing sound, as he paddled his canoe in the fast-running river that flowed past the ruins of Greystone Grange.

He woke with a start.

What's the matter with you? You look as if you've seen a ghost.

I keep dreaming about ravens. Weird, isn't it?

There's a lot of them round here. They nest in the old ruined house.

I know.

Andy clambered out of his bunk. He had to take a shower. He had to get the ravens out of his head.

Chapter Two

The current was fast and spray broke over the bow of Andy's canoe. Bill Ford, the course instructor, followed Andy.

But Andy felt as if he was part of the river itself. It was an extraordinary feeling.

There was only one other student who seemed as confident as he was. Andy had noticed her right away.

There was something very positive about Kate, Andy had noticed that when they first met. Positive and challenging.

As they rounded a bend, he looked up into the sky. With a sigh of relief he saw there wasn't the slightest sign of a raven. Why did the birds bother him so much? Why had he dreamt about them?

Bill came alongside Andy and Kate in calmer water.

Then Andy noticed an older boy paddling expertly towards them, while the other two instructors were busy rescuing students who had capsized.

Jack smiled at Kate, ignoring Andy. He had black hair and a beaky nose.

Andy felt vaguely threatened by this confident-looking boy who seemed interested only in Kate.

Andy and Kate had to struggle to keep up with him.

Following Jack as best he could, Andy looked up at the sky and saw the lone raven descending. The muscles in his arms felt as if they were going to burst as he cleaved the water with his paddle.

He could hear Kate gasping. Was she as exhausted as he was? Why didn't Jack slow down? Or was he just showing off?

Then, as they rounded another bend, Andy saw the rapids.

The current was now flowing much faster, spray flying high into the air, falling on the jagged rocks that rose glistening out of the river.
Kate was alarmed.

Jack was smiling now.

Raven Rapids are *really* menacing.

So are you, thought Andy. You even look a bit like a raven.

Andy's canoe was already bumping against the rocks and he frantically tried to fend them off with his paddle. But as he got the feel of the current he grew more confident again.

Exhilaration filled Andy and he turned to see Kate paddling behind him in a sheet of spray.

Andy's loss of concentration was fatal. As he swung back he saw his canoe was being hurled towards a jagged rock.

Then he saw a raven sitting on top of the rock.

Andy heard the loud caw above the roaring of the rapids. His canoe spun round and capsized.

Andy pushed down hard at the cockpit with his hands – and came out of the canoe like a cork from a bottle.

I'm okay.

But did Kate really care?

As the current took him, the raven flapped its wings, soaring up into the summer sky, cawing as if in triumph.

Held up by his life jacket, Andy bumped down to the bottom of the rapids. He stood up in the shallows, gasping, bruised and shaken.

He saw Jack and Kate safely in their canoes in calm water. Andy's pride was hurt.
Jack was grinning.
Kate looked worried.

Andy looked back to see the fragile craft caught behind a rock and being pounded by the current.

Andy turned away and trudged up the path beside the rapids. He felt badly humiliated.

Eventually Andy managed to grab his canoe and tow her down behind him. He slipped over several times and he could hear Jack laughing. Then he heard Kate laughing too.

I hope you haven't done any damage.

I don't think so.

Andy looked up at the sky which was clear and empty. He felt his anger boiling.

They arrived back at the centre. Jack had a proposal.

Why don't you both have a shot at the Greystone Cup?

What's that?

Andy felt stupid not knowing.

Kate was more enthusiastic.

Chapter Three

That night, there was a barbecue on the grass outside the ruined mansion.

All the members of the canoeing course sat round a blazing fire, cooking and eating sausages and beefburgers.

Know any *ghost* stories?

There was a long silence. Then Jack spoke quietly.

I wouldn't say I've got a ghost story exactly.

Then what have you got?

Jack paused.

He was staring hard at Andy, the little smile back on his lips, and Andy felt a stab of fear.

25

Jack looked down into the flames.

The Grange has always been the family home of the Dentons. They've died out now. At least most of them have and that's why the place is a ruin.

Jack looked back at the gaunt, crumbling chimneys.

Years ago, one of the younger sons fell in love with this girl. She was a stranger.

What was the guy's name?

John.

Isn't John another name for Jack?

Andy spoke without thinking. He didn't want Jack to know how much he was getting to him.

There was another long silence. Then someone called out. 'Get on with it then.'

As I said, John fell in love with this stranger – but she didn't want him. So he went mad with grief and was just about to throw himself into the rapids when he saw a young raven with a broken leg. John put the bird's leg in a splint – and eventually the raven got better.

Is that all?

No. The ravens reckoned they owed John, so when this girl found another boy to go out with, do you know what they did?

Jack paused dramatically.

The ravens attacked him. They tore out the boy's eyes and he fell into the river and drowned.

What was his name?

Andy was running beside the river and the ravens filled the sky above him, a hovering dark mass. Then they rose higher and dived. Their eyes red with rage, beaks sharp as needles.

Andy tried to beat them off but he knew his efforts were hopeless.

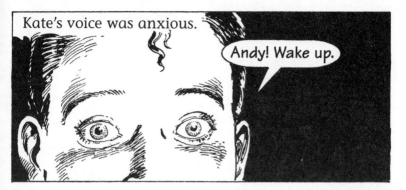

Kate's voice was anxious.

Andy! Wake up.

He woke to see the dying embers of the fire and Kate and Jack sitting together. All the others had gone to bed.

You were having a bad dream.

Kate sounded just like his mother had yesterday morning.

A *very* bad dream.

Andy felt a complete fool and staggered to his feet, embarrassed.

Sorry. I'm going to bed.

Are you sure you're all right?

I'm fine.

Not dreaming of ravens, were you?

Andy hurried away.

Chapter Four

When he woke in the early morning Andy heard shouting. Scrambling out of his bunk, he hurried outside to find Bill and Jack having a row. They were both furious with each other.

Bill gave Jack a warning glance.

Kate and Andy were practising on the rapids they had shot yesterday.

How do you feel about the Cup?

I'm not going to have any problems!

You will from me!

Then, as Andy dragged his canoe up the path for another try, he saw a single raven hovering overhead. He felt the fear pumping inside him, but he was determined not to let the bird put him off.

Reaching the top of the rapids, Andy launched his canoe. He had to do well, he had to beat Kate.

As his canoe was caught up in the current, he began to swirl past the rocks.

For a while he kept his cool, forcing himself not to look up, not to watch the raven hovering above him.

See me go!

But Andy could see the shadow of the bird on the prow of his canoe.

When he glanced up, the raven was only a few metres above his head.

Then the thing began to dive.

Suddenly his canoe was moving sideways, hitting rocks as the fragile craft began to descend the rapids, completely out of control.

At the bottom the canoe flipped over and Andy was trapped upside down. He beat with his fists at the side of the canoe.

I'm gone if someone doesn't help me!

He'd never liked eskimo rolling and the current was incredibly strong. But still no one came to his rescue and Andy was sure he was going to drown.

Help!

Water filled his mouth and he choked and gasped, still beating frantically with his fists.

Then, suddenly, the canoe was dragged away by the current and Andy found himself floundering in shallow water.

Kate was on the bank, staring down, looking terrified. Jack was beside her, watching. Andy wondered where he had come from.

You'll never get the Cup at this rate.

Jack looked guilty.

I wish I'd never heard of the Cup.

He looked up at the sky, searching for the raven.

Then Andy heard a loud cawing and saw the bird sitting on the branch of a tree that overhung the river.

The raven's eyes were piercing and Andy thought they seemed triumphant.

When they got back for lunch, Kate drew Andy aside.

That was nasty.

I felt a fool. Again.

But Kate was hardly listening.

Jack gives me the creeps.

Why?

Something about him. And he keeps asking me down to the pub.

I should go and see Bill. Will you come with me?

Now it was Andy's turn to feel triumphant.

Kate didn't enjoy telling on Jack, but she patiently explained to Bill that Jack wouldn't leave her alone.

I'll speak to him again.

He was watching Jack effortlessly rolling his canoe on the river.

Andy thought he was showing off deliberately.

I'm sorry about this. Jack's not a bad lad. Just headstrong, that's all.

Chapter Five

Bill took them out on the rapids that afternoon and Andy did much better. There was no sign of any ravens. He canoed down the rapids twice without capsizing. So did Kate.

Back in the calm of the shallows, Bill was impressed.

Well done. You both stand a chance of winning the Cup. I think we should go for the challenge tomorrow morning.

Then a dark cloud of ravens rose cawing from the ruins, soaring up towards the sun. Andy shivered and glanced at Kate. But she was looking away, staring down at the fast-flowing river.

The next day, Andy and Kate got up early to find Jack by the river. He looked agitated.

Will you take us out for a practice? The test's at eleven.

Jack grinned up at her and Andy thought he looked more like a raven than ever.

I'll take you out any time, darling.

46

Jack got to his feet, stretching lazily. He was wearing swimming shorts and the muscles in his arms bulged.

But Andy knew Jack wasn't sorry at all.

Chapter Six

Andy stared down at the damage in disbelief. Somebody had attacked his canoe with an axe.

Jack was suddenly more helpful.

49

They looked up as a lone raven began to circle overhead.

They were standing overlooking Raven Rapids, which were much wilder than the smaller rapids downstream. The current had never looked so menacing. There was a strong wind and the torrent was breaking over the rocks, sending up a misty spray. Andy looked down at his brand new canoe and sighed. He'd have to give her a go.

So you've got a vandal around here then.

We've never had any vandalism before.

Andy and Kate were sitting nervously in their canoes just above the rapids. The rest of the course had come to watch and there was a feeling of expectation. Kate's canoe was rocking gently.

A feeling of panic swept over Andy as he saw the ravens once again rising from the ruins. They seemed to be heading directly for him. Then he saw Jack. He was grinning again.

Chapter Seven

The water was coming over the bow of Andy's canoe in sheets, soaking him. Desperately steering with his paddle at high speed he found the current was pushing him through a narrow channel between the rocks.

Andy's canoe took the tight bends with long, low, sweeping movements. Just like a bird, just like a raven. A rush of confidence filled him as he swooped and glided.

The crowd was running down the steep path that ran beside the rapids, cheering and shouting. There was no sign of Jack. Then, as he got nearer, Andy saw Jack was in his canoe below, with a raven hovering over his head.

Andy's fears abruptly returned and he almost capsized, his paddle flailing, suddenly out of control.

Desperately he tried to concentrate and got some of his confidence back as he hurtled between the rocks. Somehow he avoided them all until, gasping and shaking, he met up with Jack in the calm pool below the rapids.

Soon Kate shot down to join them, raising her paddle in the air with a whoop of joy.

Amongst the cheering, Andy glanced at Jack. He was frowning.

Didn't you graze that big rock as you came down?

Andy was anxious.

No way.

Bill can vouch for that. It was a clean run for both of us.

Chapter Eight

Andy lay exhausted on his bunk. The prize-giving that evening had ended an hour ago but despite the relief at having done so well he couldn't sleep.

Jack's scornful voice repeated again and again in his head.

Then Andy heard a cawing sound and sat up in his bunk, cracking his head on the one above. Ravens didn't fly at night, did they? Shouldn't they all be in their roosts? Then he heard a light tapping sound.

Someone – or something – was knocking at the glass. Taking care not to wake the others, Andy tiptoed over to the window.

Who is it?

All he could see outside was a fluttering dark shape.

Then Andy realised he was gazing into the eyes of a raven.

Black wings flapping, the bird flew down on to the grass. In the moonlight Andy saw a figure on the lawn that led down to the river. It was Jack. Andy crept across to the door and slipped outside.

Wait a minute! I want to talk to you.

The night was warm and muggy and he thought he detected a growl of distant thunder. The raven stared up at him without the slightest sign of fear and then turned towards the figure on the lawn.

60

Jack's feet were bare and he looked as if he was sleep-walking. He was taking slow, deliberate steps and his arms were pressed to his sides.

But he didn't seem to hear. Andy began to walk quickly towards him. Jack was only a couple of metres from the river now and Andy could hear its muted roar.

Jack's eyes seemed hooded and the raven fluttered towards them.

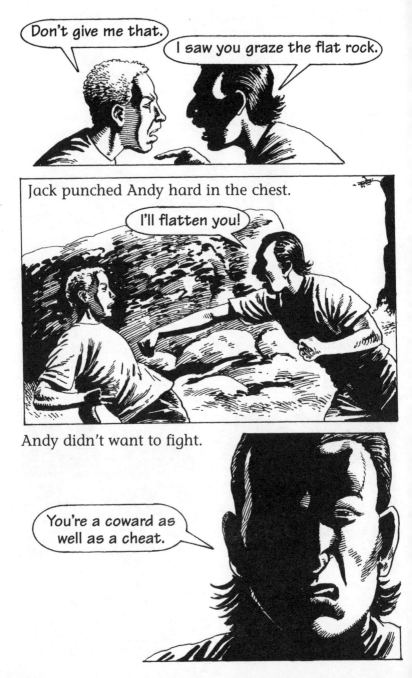

Don't give me that.

I saw you graze the flat rock.

Jack punched Andy hard in the chest.

I'll flatten you!

Andy didn't want to fight.

You're a coward as well as a cheat.

Jack hit Andy again and this time Andy lost his temper, running at Jack, fists flailing. They clinched and then, as if in slow motion, they both toppled into the lashing, foaming river.

Andy gasped as the cold water took his breath away. The current was strong and he felt weak and helpless in its grip.

He spluttered as he swallowed water and then looked round for Jack, who had just surfaced with a huge cut on his forehead that was bleeding badly.

Andy tried to strike out to reach him, but the current was much fiercer now, taking both of them down towards the Raven Rapids.

Jack!
Swim for the bank.

I can't.

His voice was weak.

The current's too strong.

Andy looked up to see a great black cloud over the face of the moon. Then the cloud began to break up.

Ravens!
The ravens are coming.

Sure enough Andy could see them now, hundreds of the birds diving down from the sky towards the rapids, coming straight at him.

The ravens are coming for you, Andy.

What?

Now they were both being whirled around in circles as the current swept them towards the bend of the river.

The ravens swooped lower. Was there something in the river they wanted, wondered Andy. Or could that something be him?

The ravens and their snapping beaks were much nearer now, just a few inches over his head.

Andy gasped and choked as he swallowed more water.

Dimly, he heard the sound of someone shouting and saw Kate and Bill running along the bank towards them.

We've got a rope.

Kate's voice seemed to come from a very long way away.

But Jack didn't reply and when Andy searched for him in the pallid moonlight he could see he was floating on his back, his eyes open and the dark blood from the gash on his forehead flowing even faster.

The rope landed in the river with a splash, but fell short.

Andy glanced up at the ravens yet again. They had risen, grouping together, making a mass cawing sound.

He began to strike out hard, doing a fast crawl, swimming towards Jack, exerting as much strength as he could against the current. But they were still being swept round the bend and Andy knew the rapids weren't far ahead.

Then he saw a tree that had fallen over the bank. If only he could push Jack into its branches then he might stand a chance of surviving. Andy knew he had to find more strength.

A raven skimmed the water, bathed in moonlight, black and powerful, beak and talons seeming to glow. In desperation, Andy struck out again, pushing Jack towards the tangle of dead branches. He managed to wedge him in the foliage and then clung on himself.

The river roared past but he knew they were both safe now.

Andy watched the ravens flying up again towards the moon.

Bill scrambled over the dead tree, grabbing Jack, pulling him gently towards the safety of the bank.

Chapter Nine

Then Bill managed to drag Andy back on land. Andy lay shivering next to Jack, who was very still. One of the other instructors was kneeling beside him, staunching the blood from the wound on his forehead.

Jack moved slightly and groaned.

Bill was calm.

We've called an ambulance but he'll need quite a few stitches.

Andy staggered to his feet as Kate moved towards him. She looked anxious.

Look at that!

Strong moonlight shone down on a young raven which was flopping about on the ground.

I think its leg's broken.

Jack opened his eyes slowly.

I'll *see* to that, I've done it before.

You'll do nothing of the kind.

Bill gently picked up the raven which struggled and then settled in his hand.

I'll fix the bird's leg and look after it until you're better. Trust me.

Jack nodded and closed his eyes again.

Bill turned to Andy. What happened?

Jack was sleep-walking and heading towards the river. I tried to stop him, but we both went in.

Bill nodded as if he understood.

I think you'll find Jack was the vandal who wrecked your canoe but I can't prove anything. He probably didn't know he was doing it.

Kate took Andy's arm and they both gazed up at the sky. The ravens were a hovering dark mass. Then, slowly, they began to flutter down to the ruins of Greystone Grange.

They're going home.

It's over.

But Andy wasn't so sure. He glanced up again. A single raven had started circling above him.